I0534345

Inciting a Write

by Rudy Thomas

ISBN 978-0-6151-5967-6

Published by Old Seventy Creek Press
Printed by Lulu Printing

Dedicated to the woman who told me
stories that became poetry

Front cover background, *The Bathers*
1877 Philadelphia Museum of Art, Mr.
and Mrs. Carroll S. Tyson Collection

Special thanks to Chelsea Sampson,
and Christy Tallent, models for back
cover

Covers designed by Gay Thomas Agee

ISBN 978-0-6151-5967-6

Starting a new work

Rain wakes me with the beat
of many hurried fingers
against the skylight.

There is ahead of the storm no heat
to fuel it. Cold air lingers
before & behind. I lie awake & write

words upon the ceiling, a page much
too large for me to fill with lines
before the rain turns it back on the world

the way a woman turns hers to the touch
of a lover's fingers grown cold. The pines,
along the creek, know her indifference

as winter soon to come.

I told a woman

to keep her eyes open
& she said: *Doing those things,
I always keep them tightly*

closed. I could not tell her why open
eyes take in the poetry sight brings
& closed eyes take in feelings. Write me

into your feelings—wind me like thread
around them & let me keep
my eyes peeled for the rhymes that go

unnoticed, I should have said.
I wished, instead, she could climb steep
Jack's Knob with me in winter when snow

blankets Upchurch hollow &
the whole of the world is a new
page unwritten & white

waiting for a poet to come down &
word feelings & images across it. To
be honest, I understood how right

she was, knowing what she was about
when her eyes were shut
but I never told her.

I wonder what

the woman thought
when I told her
her eyes were what
I needed to see.

I wonder if I ought
to have told her
her thighs were what
I needed to see

instead? There is a tree,
twisted around & up itself
& I told her I had to write
about that unusual twist.

I wonder what she
thought to herself,
that Thursday? Why write
about a tree & not mist

upon the windshield
& about the look
in her dark eyes
& not her thighs?

The answers are in the field
where tall stick weed blooms look
into clear, blue skies
& speak in sighs

as difficult to understand
as poetry is for the fat coyote.

My poetry is graphic

I say
in a hidden

sort
of way.

Those
who see

it
see me.

Those
who understand

it walk barefoot
in warm sand.

Ain't poetry
a beach?

Insects—Hot July Night

I stand on the balcony listening
to poets in the trees behind the house
to poets in the fields north,
northeast, and northwest
singing:
Life is good.
Good is night.
Night is good.
Good for life.

Perhaps the song they sing
is not the song my son hears in Iraq
nor any song a woman sings,
especially not that
of any woman I steal.
I stand on the balcony listening
until a mosquito begins to suck blood
from my naked skin.
I go inside to write words.

Perhaps I will write a song & sing it
when winter brings
its silence upon the land
& water continues its flow
the length of the valley
like a poem along a line.

The night cools

& I wake early.
I go up to the loft to be
for I have become
already
whatever poet or writer I
will ever trust to the word.

I do not have a TV
or radio in the house
to distract me with news
of the Mideast crisis Newt
predicts to be the beginning
of World War III.

I wake early
each day, most possibly
a throw back to the sum
total of my youth, steady
income, tho too little of it as I
recall, thru toil, fields & the herd.

Life demands a different fee
from each of its living—mouse,
man & woman making love, bruise
of war now or yet to come, its suit
stained red with innocent, flowing
blood. I have power only

to end this poem.

By Morning

clouds from the north & west
pushed by a cool wind
tames the built up heat.

I will go to work. I think it best
not to take a day off. I bend
to the right, to the left in my seat

& lean back, hands on my head,
my feelings weakened by a longing
I need not deny. I close my eyes.

Words pass my eyelids. I read
them like a fortune cookie: *Belonging
to a moment though it flies*

*away like a bird
is a happiness
as great as love.*

Afternoon

wind shifts westerly, forcing
a front across south central Kentucky.
After heavy rain, I drive, tires leaving
a trail on U. S. Highway 55.

Plants, wilted by a drying sun, revive.
I roll down the windows, my heart grieving
no more for flora, fauna, the unlucky
dead across the fields. There is rejoicing

I imagine. I offer all alive,
a song, as tho there are ears retrieving,
then realize if joy there is, the key
to it is rain alone—not my choice in

music, artist, a country song, *Whiskey
River* by Willie.

A finch lands on the electric

wire outside the loft bedroom where I write
& begins to sing, its alto voice clear
as aunt Ella's was in Mt. Union's choir
when I was young & impressionable.

I'm older now & impressionable
all the more in the presence of this choir
of one. It may never, Lord, come by here
again, but I stand reverent in its sight.

I am the next generation, my plight
appointed when I was born, no choir
with an Ella's voice recognizable,
singing. I applaud as its song fades in air

cooled by yesterday's rain. I say, "bravo—
bravo". In silence, the finch flies away.

In my absence

wild turkeys have claimed the woods
beneath the cliff beyond the deck.
I found a feather two days before I saw
a hen fly through the trees, upward
& land in the top of an oak.

I have
never hunted turkey
& neither shall I stalk these.
I shall not tell anyone
where this flock is.

My poem poses no danger
for the turkeys.
In the time it takes
to publish my words,
the gobbler

will have betrayed
them a hundred fold.

Facing a blank, white page

on the monitor of my computer,
I have a moment
when no words come to mind.

I close my eyes.
No words clamor to be born.
I hear night sounds,

insects singing,
their voices carried into the loft
by a cool breeze.

I walk to the screen door
& listen for a time,
but I find no rhyme,

no images I can work with.
I return to my desk chair
& close my eyes.

In front of the monitor,
words, not my own,
enter my memory:

A poet has no life
except in words.
I open my eyes & type.

There was a moon

last night & stars
no one could count for
there appeared to be no space between

them. Once, I climbed hills in early winter
& sat atop Jack's Knob alone—no light
around me except the stars,

few & far between

clouds. I felt as tho a poem
lurked in Upchurch Hollow,
words waiting to be picked up the way

my grandmother gathered eggs
from hidden nests in tall sedge
in time of bloom & blossom.

As I peered into the dark valley,
a north wind blew snow up.
It melted as quick as

it touched my cheeks.

For D. B.

I wish I knew enough to write
a novel about your life,
but I don't.

I don't
know all the details. Rife,
the ones are that I remember. The night

you drank too much and spoke
about Nam—the time they caught you
in the North & scarred your face

would be chapter three.
The time you went to a bar
would be a chapter, too.

A big man sat down beside you
& every other man moved quick, got far
back, watching. As for me,

I'd have sat calm, watching your back.
It is said you turned toward him and said,
"You must think you're tough…"

"I am tough,
tougher than you," he said
& pushed himself up & back

from the bar stool. You took an ear,
always a left ear, from your shirt
pocket & took a bite out of it

then dropped it
into the man's drink. He could not hurt
you for he was puking, but he could hear

you say:
"I didn't think
you were all that tough."

Woodpecker

does not see me, for I sit
in the garage in shadows
against the back wall.

She lands upside-down. All
at once, drilling borer bee holes,
she clucks, bills clenching a fat

larva. A young woodpecker lands
upside-down next to her
& opens its mouth to be fed.

The young bird, its head
motionless, waits beside its
mother & gets two larvae. It understands

none of the secrets
to life itself inherent in
the opening of wood.

Friends

David rode a scooter.
He was a preacher's son.

Andrew had to have a girl
if he had any fun.

Ray with his freckles—
Fay with long hair—

Jimmy loved Sue
tho she didn't care...

Buz was the brain
who made things spin.

Phyllis was puzzling
to Mitchell & Ben.

Linda & Carrie
would play jacks & sing.

Donnie & Terry
got into everything.

We played for a time
then scattered like leaves—

some far from the source—
some close to the trees.

For the woman who would rather be Venus

rising from sea foam—
naked, & without shame—
than relive her youth—I write.

She need not settle for Venus imperfect
tho her hair is too short to cover her
breasts, them too small for some men

to covet tho not so small others will not
want to touch them & part her thighs,
drooling for her poetry,

& like a butterfly in orange glow,
move about, then take a too long recess
in the emptiness of her arms.

Hummingbird

He's a multicolored one,
bigger than the rest,
& mean tempered.

I have watched him
since the first blooms
of spring began.

Now that leaves begin
their falling off & down,
I understand

how it is that the smallest
of the females—
those willing to do anything

for water sweet as nectar—
can empty the feeder
with his blessing.

Poet at Night

I saw a Blue Jay in sunlight
high above me
in the oak,

opening acorns,
indifferent to my presence,
his thoughts occupied

by the fruit of the tree.
As for me
& as for poetry,

I cannot write words
to praise his purpose
tho his hunger like mine

is real, but so different.
If I had to write words at all,
on this night,

I would find them
in the uppermost branches
of your eyes.

I hear my voice

in this place where I sit
in morning shadows beneath a cliff.
It whispers words the way the wind
whispers.
It is joyful, leaping like the water
of Old Seventy Creek over the falls.
It sings like finches in the Chestnut Oak
above me.

My voice is a poem.
No one hears the silence of it.
No one sees the subject of its words.
No one cares whether I write the bird's
song or wrap emptiness into an image
of a blue Forget-Me-Not in bloom
or of a woman dancing naked
in front of her mirror.

For Stewart Parrish

I cannot remember whether I read it
or whether someone told me:
every woman lives
within her own parenthesis.

My grandfather & I talked about women
and horses on his front porch in
Richmond, Ohio
when he was past ninety.

His insight into horses
spilled out of him in words
so full of feelings
that he spoke a spellbinding poetry.

Equally fascinating were his words:
every woman has a story that begs
to be written—
a dance in her walk that begs for music—

a song in her heart
to wreck the fleetest ship
& more mystery in her eyes
than any man can steal.

"I have known some," he said
& we sat there in silence
for a long time before I understood
that he meant in a Biblical sense.

Thoreau

came to mind
when I saw you pass--
looked into your eyes gazing back at
mine, green, alive as Walden's pond early
      in spring would have been.

      His words find
me & gather my feelings into one mass:
**The question is not what you look at,
but what you see**.
Perhaps I see more than other men

      have. Perhaps I see you as you
see yourself--stronger than your voice
& the curves of your body
would have men believe.
I see you unfold like a flower, quiet,

      vibrant. My Poem wants you
in it the way Thoreau's woods of choice
longed ever for individuality
& perpetual youth. My eyes do not leave
yours willingly. I am day, resisting night.

In my loft

I sit with only the light
from the computer monitor
interrupting the dark.

I sit waiting to write,
my thumb beneath my chin or
my fist against my cheek. Dogs bark

toward the northeast wood.
Insects sing a song, letting words go,
upward, outward, thru the trees.

What I understand, I understood
first on Old Seventy Creek in its flow,
water up to my knees.

The wind

in the trees, threatens rain
or a late July storm tho
my grandfather always said:
It seldom rains at night in July.
It teases like a woman
during long hot days & drops,
large & few, or a fine mist falls.

I sleep without AC, insect calls
fill the room. I do not know
when the wind lays. I wake in the dead
of night, the room too cool. I
hear the rain begin slowly. No woman,
teasing, is it. It stops
then pours down. It is the rain

parched goldenrods rejoice in &,
no doubt stems heavy with bloom perk
up & frogs croak along the creek
as tho it is April. All night,
the rain visits welcome as a lover.
I lie awake, feelings elated,
thoughts tuned fine for words.

I begin to write the words
across my memory, rejuvenated
as tho I am a flower long parched. I cover
myself, dream & write
images of past embraces—the peak
of Jack's Knob & unusual women lurk-
ing in the rekindled depths of my soul &

rainfallsdown&downwithneverapause.

For Dareck

I ask you if you want to drive the Corvette
& I see a look that pleases me
as you shout for Teresa, your wife.

You give her your camera
& speak Polish. She comes
to the passenger's side of the car.

"You have made him happy,"
Teresa says. "He loves cars.
He wants a picture."

I offer him a small bottle
of Maker's Mark.
"I don't drink," he says.

"It is a souvenir," I say,
"made in Kentucky."
Teresa shoots a picture, then another.

"Souvenir?" he repeats.
"Then I will take it. Thank you."
I measure with my hands

to tell him the car is low on the ground.
He nods.
"Three," he asks, shifting.

"Unless you want to back up,"
I say, "then it's R.
"Can't I go?" he asks, motioning forward.

"Yes," I answer
"Lights?"
I point toward the pull switch.

He drives slowly the length of the drive.
Out of the gravels, he speeds up.
"How old?" he asks.

"Twenty-five years old," I answer.
"It is old," he says,
"but it has character. I have a BMW 7..."

"A good car," I say.
"Left?" he asks at HWY 1590.
"Straight," I point across the highway.

"It is fast," I say of the Corvette,
"without," I make a motion like a snake
& continue: "fast where it is straight."

I know he will test it.
He does, up the straight hill
beyond the bridge.

The Corvette roars,
squeaks tires,
Dareck smiles.

"Thank you," he says
as he turns into Eddie
& Fay's driveway.

"You are welcome,"
I assure him.

"You can't write,"

he said,
"about me & use names,
but in Vietnam
when I left there in '73
when we were pulling out,
I'd say there were only—
as far as I know—7
true snipers.

Sniper schools,
training as such,
started later for the Navy.
I was a marine.
My MOS was truck driver.
With a weapon, you got
classified:
marksman, sharpshooter,
& expert.

After boot camp,
I got a chance to do—
how should I say—
got asked if I wanted
to learn to blow up things—
demolition--& I said yes.
Then someone looked
at my record—saw I was an expert
with a rifle. That's how it began.

Now Vietnam wasn't like you see it
in the movies. It wasn't John Wayne
shooting at men coming head on...
If you can imagine firing from the head,
sweeping jungle, it was more like that
in a *Fire Fight.*
You see, there was a lot of jungle killed
there.
You learned to tape your clips together
so you could flip one over
& you learned never to shoot empty.
An empty rifle makes a different sound
than one that's loaded.
An empty rifle locks back
& you have to take time to fill the
chamber.
Lots of grunts never lived long enough
to know that's why they died.
If they heard that empty,
they'd rush the sound of it.
We got issued 100 round clips.
When you tossed empties on the ground,
you wanted to have 4 or 5 rounds left
in the clips if you got to gather them up
later. You pick up a clip with only 1 round
in it & you could count yourself lucky.
You learned to judge by sound 100
rounds.

Now my gun,
when they decided to use me,
was a 308 Browning automatic someone
had reworked the stock
& painted it black—the whole thing
painted black.

The longest jungle kill to my knowledge
was 1268 feet—confirmed
in that
the man was lying on the ground
afterwards.

I'd say 90% of the time
I got flown 80% of the way,
if you know what that means
& it got so I was having fun,
enjoying myself.
Once, I came back after four months,
& had to go to the commanding general's
house.
He looked at me—
I dressed like I wanted—
in my hat & asked me:
& you say you are a marine?
I said: **yes sir**
& he told me to call my parents.
It seems my things got sent home
& I was supposed to be MIA, dead.
The old man had raised so much cane
wanting to know how I died
that I had to call.
I talked to mom & dad for an hour.
How do you talk to your parents
that long?

Some times, I'd come in
& nobody'd know where to send me.
One time they sent me back
to my company
& it had changed so much
no one knew me.

I reported with orders to get my things
& stay for no more than a week
then go out again.
There was a green 2nd lieutenant in charge
who no doubt had never been in a *fire
fight.*
When I told him who I was,
he didn't like the way I looked
& he let on like my belongings
had been sent to HQ.

I told him HQ sent me to get my things
& he told me I'd have to check with
supply.
I did.
Supply had them, but only one outfit.
I asked where my other outfit was
& it turned out the 2nd lieutenant took it.
I went straight to him—asked why he took
it.
He told me I only got one outfit.
I told him I always got two outfits—that
HQ had sent me to get mine & I'd have
them.
He threatened me. Said I'd be up on
charges as soon as he called HQ.
XO came up then, a colonel, & looked at
me—called me by name & asked: *you back
here?"*

"Only for a week," I told him, "then I'm out
again."
"I'm bringing him up on charges," the
lieutenant began...

"You don't want to do that!" the XO said.
"As soon as I get to communications," he said…
XO cut him off with a salute—looked at me & asked," Didn't I see you with officer's stripes higher than this soldier last time you were here?"
"Yes, sir," I assured him.
"What's your rank now?" he asked.
"You'll have to call HQ to find out," I said.
"You go to communications & find out," he ordered, "then come back & tell us."

When I came back, XO asked,
"what did they tell you?"
"Told me there was a change in plans," I said. "I'm going out at 2400 hours tonight."
"Bullshit!" the lieutenant shouted. "How you plan to do that! You're in the middle of the jungle where night is black."
"You're to give me my things," I told him.
"Get them!" XO ordered.
The lieutenant left—came back with both outfits.
He said, "He ain't going nowhere tonight. Tomorrow, I'm bringing him up on charges & it's the brig for him."
XO looked at me & asked, "What're we going to do about this problem?"
"Send him out with me & I'll solve your problem," I said.
"You'll get him killed," he said.
"I won't get him killed," I said, "but he won't come back."

"At midnight, I walked out of the canopy
& dropped my little light on the ground.
Lieutenant came out cursing.
Before he could finish yelling how he was
going to have me up on charges,
a ladder dropped down,
I stepped on it & was gone."

"When they brought us out,
I had 130 days or so left to serve.
They were letting everybody go—those
with 120 to 130 days like me.
They said I was critical—sent me to NC
to guard tanks.
When I had 2 or 3 days left, I asked to go
home. They told me I had longer than
that.
I made them look.
They sent me home—said I was classified
as critical & wanted to know how a truck
driver gets classified as critical.
I told them I blew up things."
The Colonel in charge said," & more!"
"He was the same man I knew from Nam,
but there he was known as Mr.—no! You
can't write his name! In the States a
Colonel, but in the jungle Mr. _____...
He called the shots both places..."

"When I'd been out a short time, a Navy
man called me, raising hell... Said I'd
never served my time. I hung up on him.
He called back. I hung up. He called back

every day & told me he was sending for
me. I told him to punch my name in his
database. He did. Said it showed I hadn't
served my time. I told him to punch my
name into his database."

He did.
"Now what?" he asked.
"Type in the code 290672," I said.
He did.
"What the hell did you do!" he yelled.
"I'm sorry, I'll have to call you back."

"When he called back the next day,
he kept apologizing
& saying he didn't know.
They came & got me several times
after that. We'd fly out
& stand down.
That's how it was for me. You see,
someone always remembered I was critical
when they needed me."

In a Time Before Writing

our eyes met.
I sensed what I have sensed
in other places,
the scent of a poem.

An affair of feelings, such poems
are &
nothing less.
If she should meet

me again by chance,
me clothed in words—
she reading them, I wonder:
will she catch her breath,

glance
up from her poem,
remembering,
or simply turn the page?

To Satisfy My Brother-in-law

I will write a poem about a woman
& he will think it is a poem
about a particular woman on a houseboat

or he will imagine her
to be a stripper
or some woman I was able to steal

talking literature
& writing words—so—
in order to satisfy him—

I will write a poem about the open
book in her eyes
& he will imagine a woman

tri-sexual,
willing to tryanythingsexual,
& imagine her naked

on a houseboat beneath the Falls
or lap dancing in an A-frame...
I will not paint idle scenes

I will let my poetry portray her as she is
tho he might imagine her one
of the women he suggests

either one making love
across these lines & down the page
full of possibilities

He would have me write
as tho he alone
has opened my mind

with scissors
as were it a door lock
he has jimmied

to look inside
& I will write him as being awed
by what he sees the woman

doing there

Unique woman

She takes pride
in her liberal slant on life.
She is neither weak nor wanting
nor any man's toy.

Thunder
beyond the north wood
& wind threatening
& a sky, dressed in a black

evening gown,
take control of my poem.
She makes it difficult for poets
to write about her sensual side.

Low to the right,
above the trees, a flash,
white edged in blue,
strikes the ground.

Waves of rain cross the field.
I have no means,
other than poetry,
to describe her, the storm

or how my imagination
weaves itself
around a blank line
as tho it were a woman.

Her poem

Before I climb to the loft,
intent on being poet enough
to write her poem,
I sit in my chair,
& stare thru a wall of glass.

Hummingbirds fight to protect
their feeders.
The feeders,
the fighters, the wind in the trees
are not her poem.

Her poem must be made
of particulars like wings beating air
to hover; be something that touches her—
a song—something as uninhibited
as two squirrels copulating

in the white maple.

Finally

one squirrel came down
the white maple
& crossed the low limb
toward the deck.

Dropping silently
more than a foot,
it ran along the rail,
tail beating excitedly.

It had discovered
the ear of corn,
held upright by a nail
on the new feeder

& scolded it
as it has scolded me
from the white maple,
hidden behind green leaves.

The Storm

I will send her a lightning bolt
filled with good wishes,
words for a song,
& money enough to end
her frustrations.

Having no control over it,
I cannot say when it will reach her
for it moves from cloud to cloud
across the sky & all that is certain
is the fact that it will strike down.

It will not hit her
nor even come close
for it is not meant to do harm.
What she chooses to gather up first
will say the most about her.

Riddle

Black on white;
white ( )
& black
straps to knees—

what is it?

If you give up,
count to ten
& I will tell you
I have forgotten

the answer.

Old Seventy Creek, September

Wind rustles leaves,
& some drop early
like a dancer's wraps.
Trees sing songs of frost,
& the hot sun
grows less miraculous.
Winter sits in the audience,
waiting for a lap dance.

Late September Moon

centered above Jack's Knob
is only the right side
of an incomplete parenthesis

bright it is against the high peak
& I feel a poem, a tide
of desire overtake me

& imagine poetry
especially its unseen side
then imagine how desire

makes a man greater
than a mountain
& greater than the moon

centered above it

The pet

My grandfather
a lifetime before I was born
caught a young, red fox pup
& took it home
to tame it

He named the fox
Red Fox
& tied it to a stake
& put a dog house
next to the stake

Red Fox grew
eating table scraps
& as the story goes
grew fox wise
in the process

Red Fox would scoot
his feed pan with his nose
to a point inside the circle
his feet made
at the end of his chain

& lie down
to wait for my grandfather's hens
to feed on the scraps
& that is how he ate
half of the flock

before grandfather took him
to Jack's Knob
& released him.

When Picasso made

pencil thin charcoal lines,
his sketches used the white spaces
of a canvas the way a poet
uses the page to create a work.

Picasso worked with many models
but loved one at a time more than
all of them each time he sketched,
painted, posed them & touched them

to capture the essence of their faces,
their soft breasts, their lips & hips,
bend of an elbow, length of a smile,
or an eyelid closing,

& as he grew in art
he began to take apart
the human form & put it on canvas
the way he wrote poetry

When critics pressed him to explain
his work,
he simply stated:
All art is erotic.

Renaissance Hotel, St. Louis

As I insert the plastic key
into the door lock
with the arrow pointing down
I hear a woman

in the next room
cry out in pleasure
& I smile
unable to imagine

how she looks
I do not take her voice
to be one in a low budget film,
never in sync with lips

My smile like April new growth
along the banks of Old Seventy Creek
one woman would say
happened for a reason

The unseen woman
her voice
her passion
are things irrelevant

When I write, words cross the page
like water emerging from underground
to feed the flow of a wild Kentucky creek
along its winding course toward a waterfall

The woman drives thru

her neighborhood
pointing out the house

where her parents live
the pay lake

the house where her boyfriend lived
only its blue roof visible

the house where a crazy man
& his crazy wife live—her on the porch

the house where a young man lived
who stalked her

confessed his love for her
told her he was gay

then killed himself the same night
& as she drives past

The Loving Hands Baptist Church
she tells the story of a young man

who wanted her to park there
so they could have their way

with each other
but she would not

for she thought it wrong
& he begged her to take them

49

to her school
& she said the cops would come

but he insisted
so she drove there

parked
& they walked to a white shed

& the police came
like she said they would

they watched two officers shine lights
into the car & check her tag

watched them leave
then raced to the softball field

climbed the fence
& crossed the diamond to the dug out

where they did whatever it was
they did to each other

& as they started back
a second cop car came

shined light into her car
checked her tag

& drove away

As she drives

she tells me
about waking up

seeing the light
in her bathroom

& closing her eyes
telling herself

I'm dying
telling herself

I'm not ready
& opening her eyes

looking away from the light
thinking

I don't want to go yet
& in the half-light

seeing the ironing board
across the room & saying to herself

Oh my God
it's Jesus

& as she drives & talks

her left hand drops
her fingers become a poet
writing
slowly
slowly
& I become a reader

my eyes are a sinkhole
her words flow thru me
like water

Inciting a write

She stands—raises her arms
her sweat shirt rides up

She stretches
arms still up

balances tip toe
Her sweat pants

slide so
revealingly low

that in the space
between the black of up & down

her white skin is a blank page
& I long to touch it with words

left to right
before she catches me

but I can neither place the song
of a quail there

nor the rustle of oak leaves
on Jack's Knob in early winter

nor the excited locating bark
of a black-and-tan hound

beneath Sewell Bluff
& tho her white skin

is aesthetic enough
to contain those sounds

those images and more—
Renoir's *Bathers*—

Mermaids—
all of Old Seventy Creek

from its rising to its fall
into the blue green headwaters

of Lake Cumberland
the eternity of the moment ends

her arms drop
she tugs her pants

triumphant
& with no obvious concern

for poetry
turns away

The moon in the morning

low against the horizon
& bright before day break

had the look
of a poem

about it
& an owl flew

out of darkness
thru its light

into darkness again
leaving nothing

of itself
In passing

leaving
everything

There is no joy

in her face
tho the day is bright

The sky has no end
to the blue of it

Void of poetry
she wears stress

in dark circles
beneath her eyes

& I feel
a chill

tho October sunlight
warmer than usual

sings of love
across the lawn

& the only thing I can do
is exist

silent as a stone
in Old Seventy Creek

She stands before me

& I cannot look into her eyes
for they do not look back

I look down as she folds
& unfolds the waist band

of her jeans

I feel her eyes
tho she yet

looks down
intently

works relent(less)ly
while I smile & write silently

I know she is aware
of my watching yet

her fingers expose
the whitest of her skin

I have no idea
what she thinks

I am writing
in those brief moments

when my mind & feelings
are dancing partners

Rain falls

& I am reminded of how
I could not write
did not write four
five
perhaps six days

frost has now
painted maples red, the sight
of one of them like a woman more
alive
than when sun rays

ruled & grass grew
toward the sky
the time those
maples hid their beauty—
even to the one—behind green

the voice of rain runs thru
me like a poetry my
soul must not compose
a poetry not written to be
or mean

anything
but everything & all
the time the rain sings it
as it falls

I search the hills again

but the poem I look for
eludes me
like a wild turkey

It hears my eyes walk by
dry leaves crunching or
a twig snapping under the
weight...

But wait—I know those
hills for
they are your eyes
& the poem is there

Know this: it is so inciting
that I catch my breath
when it spreads wings
& rises whistling thru the trees

I tell the woman

how to approach my words
& she nods

What I do not tell her
is how I never tire

of the mystery that I see
in her eyes

I do not tell her
that feeling comes first

then seeing comes

In the dark tonight
I stand above the cliff

listening to coyotes howl
toward Old Seventy Creek

I sing so softly
that even the chipmunks

asleep in their dens
warm in their bed of leaves

can not hear me
& shiver with fear

shiver like the woman
did today when the cold wind

ate thru her clothing
feeding upon her warmth

with no intention
of waking desire

The wind's voice thru the trees
says to me: *Fool*

*Who are you to think
that you can challenge me*

I answer:
I am the fool

*gathering twigs
to build a fire*

Waking

The room is dark
& the sky beyond the wall
of glass like the woman's eyes
is darker—no sound--no stars &

clouds mark
distance, space, the face of the all.
The poet tries—
imagines &

paints words, a meadow lark,
cold in fescue, Seventy-Six Falls
where it drops down, the whys
&

wherefores of life, love, stark
naked feelings, tall
as oaks caressing skies.
Waking, wanting the warmth of skin

&
being not indifferent to desire,
he rises
& builds a different fire.

I lean against a doorway

& watch the woman,
her head keeping time to music
as she works

& tho I think I should slip
quietly away,
I stay where I am.

I am reminded of a sparrow hawk
that sits above the bird feeder
& drops without a sound

to capture a yellow finch
while it eats from a feeder
on the railing.

I am no hawk, but hawk like,
I seek words to feel my emptiness.
She is a most unlikely muse

for she gives shape to her own words,
the shape of a song,
sharp notes to music.

She looks up, almost startled,
& I only have the start of a poem
to hide behind.

Driving thru fog

I can not see Lake Cumberland
tho I travel above it on Wolf Creek dam.

Lake to my right,
river to my left,

& both do not exist
for the moment.

Driving thru fog,
I appreciate the rolling hills

covered with hard wood
& pine

& I come to an understand-
ing as to how limited I am

as man alone—how when I write
there are no limits to my words. To my left

river
& to my right lake

& both exist
in that moment

for I imagine them as they would
be in sunshine

& in that moment I remember the infinite
distance there is within a woman's eyes.

Out of the fog

along Hwy 55
I see fields of fescue

white with frost
& I hear the crunch

my feet have made
in such conditions

sometime ago.

Out of the fog,
a spike buck leaps

& stops in the road
confused.

I brake;
stop too; &

the deer leaps
out of the road

into a ravine
& disappears.

A New Poem

lives inside me, a poet
as hollow as a sycamore.

It
hides beneath more

brown leaves than it should
& sleeps. It has rhythm & feet

that do not drum wood—
a sound easily mistaken for the heartbeat

of a timid squirrel when a hunter's ear
rests against the tooth scarred entrance,

but it is not a heartbeat. Hear
me! Its sound is not a heartbeat.

A poem dreamed me

last night.
The sofa opened &
the poem would not
emerge.

The
poem's voice, demonic, thru tight
clenched teeth &
guttural growls, would not
emerge.

The back of the easy chair
split, another bottomless pit,
horizontal, & tempted me,
like a woman does, her eyes
beautiful as Old Seventy Creek in sunlight

& such a remarkable silent stare.
I could neither lure it
out nor allow the poem to take me
in. The openings closed. A bat tries
to embrace a full moon. I watch its flight

until it becomes a speck in the distance.

Half moon bright

toward the southern sky,
an eye, not a woman's,
looking back at the world
without blinking
gets me thinking—
makes me remember the azure
sea off Poros, Greece in June
& the first time the woman
caused me to look away,
smile,
nod my head as tho
I knew what she knew
about poetry.

One half moon bright as an eye
is not a poem. One woman's
look is not a million rhymes, unfurled
lines, or too many stars, winking,
thru autumn leaves for thinking
man or feeling poet to pursue.
I write, instead, a moon
as bright as day
in its breaking while
wild geese fly slow
& certain thru
it in a V.

Yesterday, today

I have been without your silent stare
I have been unable to enter into words
I have been without their sound
I have been unable to touch them

Poetry must happen to me
the way Old Seventy Creek,
in its rush of water toward the falls,
happens to me

or the way your eyes happen to me
their mixed signals
like a line
ending

When your eyes blink

the thought I have
keeps on
flowing like Old Seventy Creek
across the landscape
of my mind

Emerging from the Sinks
the water gathers speed
pooling for a moment
as it tries to turn
back on itself
but it can not return
nor can I

When your eyes open
again, I am
Old Seventy Creek
beyond the edge
of the limestone cliff
falling upon fish in Lake
Cumberland with no notion of

or feeling for such trivial
pursuits

There are times

after these many years
when I can close my eyes
& see the house I am in
explode
black the air becomes
& thick
the millions of particles
swirling
mingle with other houses
& move over the hill
taking trees
& cars
toward Lake Cumberland

I can see my daughter
in the fireplace
crying
& my Gibson guitar
sticking out of debris
its music silenced

forever

Saturday Morning

November mist in my face...
Oaks stand on rolling KY hillsides bare
as strippers, their leaves g-strings
tossed on a stage. The wind, a
John, whistles across the black sky.

I walk to the creek; trace
a brown stone with my finger; & stare
into the water. A finch sings
as tho it is May.
In your eye,

once, in a place
such as this, I dare
say, I saw the stain glass wings
of a
dragonfly.

Woman in a Mexican restaurant

I should not have looked at you
when you leaned back in your chair,
arms up—not in the way I did.
I should not have thought about a creek,
Old Seventy, in that moment,
but I did. The creek mirrors shadows
& sunlight thru hardwood trees,
naked in winter, to stress the worthiness
of life. My eyes loafed at ease in the
manner of Walt Whitman & much too far.

I remember watching two
hawks coming in toward the creek, their
wings unmoving like a poem hid-
den in your eyes. I am a poet. The creek
is but water cold & moving, invent-
ing the illusion that shadows
move. Where the sycamore trees
lean out & over it & below the surface less
than the thickness of cloth covering the
rise of your breasts, there is a gravel bar.

Before the poem

in her eyes asked me to write it,
I was a poet, blind &
listening for words with one good ear.

I suppose I expected it
would be a song vibrant &
clear like a finch sings in & near

Old Seventy Creek or up near
the top of Jack's Knob when &
if a poem came to me, but it

came to me, silent as a tear.
The touch of her eyes cured me &
I saw it.

I may never write it,
but I saw it &
it was mirror clear.

& tonight writing

after two days of unseasonable warmth
I remember how warm a woman feels
tho I only dream

she is on top & we are not lovers
I know that much
she wears a stranger's face

nothing else about her is unfamiliar
but her face looking down on me
is unfamiliar

she smiles bends forward
& blows her breath
hot it is

upon my neck
but when she touches me
where she does

her fingers are cold as death
& I wake
I remember listening to the wind outside

I remember watching leaves cross the deck
like field mice
& then the rain begins to fall

a mist at first
then large drops
against the windows

On nights like this

the old urge returns
I close my eyes
I am on Old Seventy Creek
My hounds trail a raccoon
Its footprints in the mud
by the bank
& their footprints go upstream

Eyes still closed
I take off my glove
& put my fingers in the cold water
As it flows thru them
I envy its forever going
downstream toward the falls
& I write a tribute to it on the only
piece of wood that drifts by

Family Reunion

It would be hot,
& usually dry when we
traveled north to Ohio
to meet my mother's family
at a park, a lake, or near a creek.

I wake mornings & seek
another trip up I-75 to hilly
land she called home. Ohio
is 11 steps down now—pictures on the
wall above the sofa. Those to the left not

Buckeye relatives, but KY kin.
I shift my gaze to the right, at the top
my mother & her brother in uniform.
Beneath them, her oldest brother, dead
more years than my youngest child has
breathed life.

Lower down, is a portrait, a study in strife,
my grandparents, a robust woman, head
& shoulders above the short form
of a man, them posed with horses. Drop-
ing down, the oldest portrait, circa 1910

of a woman, my maternal treat-
grandmother, poverty etched in her eyes,
etched by the holes in her sweater—she
endures on the wall, defying death awhile
in the family tree I planted.

Between the right & the left tree—slanted,
always—my paternal great-
grandparents, Civil War era, no smile
on either, survivors, KY transplants. The
TN, NC, VA & German skies

of their families unseen. My father sits
upon a make believe wall in uniform &
his parents' picture beneath his own
is not their best—the man after a stroke,
the woman yet strong, standing tall.

The tree has group pictures, all
leaves, & bare limbs where hangers broke
& not enough space for the hundreds gone
farther than the living travel &
return, sent toward an uncertain eternity
in well pressed outfits.

November 17, 2006

I drive across the street
to the left from the Brown Hotel
drive along an alley
turning right
drive along another long alley
then turn right into a parking lot
of five stories
taking a ticket so the gate will raise
I turn right again into an area
where I can not park
for each space is reserved

After I turn around
for there is no way out
or up
I start out & a woman motions
me out of the compound
blocks the way up
& I have to tell her I want to park

Annoyed
she tells me I'll have to go up
which I knew already
& I wait for her to move so I can

Half way between levels 1 & 2
I see a parking space to the left
but I can not take it
cars on either side
parked over the lines
leave no space for another vehicle

Three spaces from level 2
I park
get out
lock the doors
& climb stairs to the 3rd level
where there are doors with a sign:
Employees Only

I take the stairs to level 4
no exit
then climb to level 5
the rooftop lot

I take the elevator to level **G**
& find an outside door
opening on the long alley
I must walk until I turn left
then walk straight thru an alley
to the street
which I cross to enter the **Brown Hotel**

In the hotel
I take an elevator to the 16th floor
the **Gallery** where W. S. Merwin will read
& I am almost three hours early
but I have traveled far
& it has taken me since 1965
when I first discovered the poet's words
taken me that long
to get to a place where he would read
& I want to be on the first row

After I have been alone for an hour,
I hear the service elevator,
the rattle of dishes behind me.
A woman in a black uniform pushes
a cart loaded with plates
from behind the wall & looks at me.

Do you know where I am supposed
to set up the coffee
& snacks she asks

I do not I answer

She leaves
returns later with two men
dressed in black
The men carry the tables from the back
of the room into the hallway outside the
Gallery

Is this where the poetry reading will be
I hear a woman ask one of the workers
I do not hear an answer
I'll ask him
I hear the woman say & I turn
I motion to the young woman & nod my
head

It's still an hour & a half before it starts
the young woman says as she walked
down the aisle
I hitched a ride with a friend
who's going to a concert

From where I ask

UK she answers
I'm a student there

Are you a writer I ask

If you ask everyone here tonight
if they write
they'll say yes she said
Do you write she asked
I hand her a copy of my book
Is that you she points at my name
I nod
She sits two seats from me & reads
After a time of silence she says
You are a writer
She reaches toward me
Keep it I say
Thanks she replies
People are starting to come in now
she says
I'm going to see if I can get a cup of coffee
Leave your things I tell her
Thanks she says & leaves

A woman rushes to the podium
looks on it
looks inside it
looks frightened
& leaves

The room becomes noisy
The woman rushes back to the podium
a large man in a black uniform following
close on her heels

This won't do she blurts out
No desk light
No water
Not enough chairs

The man takes out his cell phone
& barks orders
Soon another man dressed in black
brings water
a desk lamp
& turns to leave

Chairs the woman cries out
looking back from the podium
You asked for 200 chairs the large man
assures her
How many did you set up she demands
The second man begins to count
not one by one
but row by row
After he finishes he returns
199 chairs he tells the woman
plus 1 for the recorder there
pointing to the front & left of the hall

This won't do the woman
frantic
says
There are 103 of us
He is a popular poet
There will be other poets here as well
We want them on the front with him
& we don't know how many from outside
will be here she continues
looking at me & the young woman's purse

on the floor
her jacket on the back of the chair
& I know she means me
& the absent young woman
who is a student
& I nod toward her
but I do not get up
as she hoped I would

She rushes out
followed by the two men in black
& shortly three more men in black
roll carts of stacked chairs down the aisle
The room is almost full I see
as I look toward the back
The men hurry
set four rows of chairs in front of me
They leave
The young lady returns
a cup of steaming purple brew in her
hands
Are we moving up she asks
I was watching your things
I'm moving I say
I'm following she says

The woman returns
turns on the desk lamp
fills a glass with water
puts the glass on a shelf
inside the podium
& looks at us
outsiders
We do not move
Her mouth drops open

I turn
W. S. Merwin walks down the aisle
followed by a large group of the 103
chosen ones
& the frantic woman says something
to the people in the front rows opposite us
but they move

Sena Jeter Naslund introduces the poet
& he begins to read
& every poem he reads
I have read
I remember his words
for I have hung onto them
like a skylark hangs onto the sky
but his voice is new
He reads
the flow iambic
& perfect
no cracking
no drinking from the glass

She tells me a story

& the tragedy of it is this
that it is a story
about a house

the house where she lives
at least where she has a bed
& sleeps if

they let her
the other two women
in the story

& it is not so much
a story about a house
as it is a tale

about the wicked things
the other two women
her friends

who are not her friends
do
to make her want to leave

or make her return
if she goes out
do things

like telephone her
& tell her to come home
before the movie is over

tell her
they will lock her out
& tell her not to wake them

if the door is locked
when she gets back
& they will not give her a key

& when she goes away
to a distant city to a friend's house
mid-week

the two show up
late at night
& bring their dog

a dog that can not learn
but the story
is not about the dog

so when I write
it down
I will write a poem

about the woman's
soft lips forming the words
& I will exclude

the two women with hearts black
as her hair is black
against white skin

When he drank

my father who would fight at the drop of a
hat mellowed & made light of his condition
a man who loved women & sang songs to
them—danced, high-stepping, across their
hearts when he drank
drank bourbon by choice with its mix of
grains—its limestone spring water
or drank moonshine with his friends

Once when he drank alone on Lake
Cumberland, he claimed he saw a
mermaid below the Falls
swimming she was
swam right up to his boat
& asked for a drink
& he shared his Makers with her
& she shared her story
there on the front of his wooden
square nosed boat

& when she drank enough to feel
she took his reel & fished
her hook baited with a scale she peeled
from her slender lower half
he said
but all she managed to catch
the entire afternoon
was his complete
& undying attention

At Churchill Downs she said

if I tried to walk in those
pointing at their stilettos
I'd fall flat

& I'd not be caught out here
dressed like that either
she says
watching the two blondes

when they sat she notices
they're holding hands
behind their programs
& no one cares

I don't care
I say
& you don't care
either

I've noticed them in bars
she says *with their long hair—*
foxy—good looking ladies
They call them lipstick lesbians

Is that the latest trend
I ask
yes
she says

they're an item
& no one cares
but if I tried that in public
everyone would be up in arms

I am a people watcher she says
I am, too I agree *that's how I write poetry*
thinking how I prefer the crowd
to the clubhouse on a day so warm

I smell beer
& perfume
& horse manure
& listen to the drunken man

above us rant
The handlers lead
the thoroughbreds past us
toward the paddock

I hear the obnoxious man
shout something about confirmation
the breeding of one of the horses
& the money it has won

I watch the gray horse
& I will bet on it as I always do
then I watch the poetry in her eyes
walk about & I see her smile

I think about the race
she is running
in search of herself
& I wish for her a horse

wild eyed—head held high
one that leaves the others
at the starting gate & runs
while she rides it never looking back

Watching Old Seventy Creek flow

at dawn
along & down its course toward the falls,
I am alone on a wooden bridge.
In the water I see light below
glow as I have seen it in your eyes.

If I am anything, I am wise
enough in the silence to know
how poetry moves along the ridge
of feelings like a fox or swims the squalls
upstream like a Red Horse in its spawn.

The fence

I walk along the sloping
path toward the head
of the hollow

where beech & oak tower
& when I come to the rock fence
few have seen

I stop.

He was a free slave
my father's voice speaks
from the grave—

telling me at a time when I am young
& hunting with him at night
& while the hounds strike a trail

near the ancient bear wallows
the story.

He gathered these stones
& laid one upon the other
around this small tract of land
he bought.

His house was there I see him pointing
in the middle of it.
Then he says
Nothing remains of the man

save this rock fence
& the silence that is death.

& when a reader asks me

who is the woman
What do I say
say she is only the woman
who is not

say instead
she is a muse taking life
say she is both woman
& muse

& when another reader asks me
who is the woman
should I say nothing
or say read the poetry

say catch her silent stare
the red sky of morning
in her eyes
or evening shadows there

say catch Old Seventy Creek
its quick splash & ripple
with cupped hands
until your fingers chill

& if still
you do not know her
like fog on a warm morning
she will disappear before your eyes

Eye of the Beholder

I open my eyes some days
& the haze concealing
Old Seventy Creek clears,
fog lifted. Singing, yellow
finch fears not the sound
his voice makes thru the trees.
Minnows go round & around, their
circling quick, silent as pain.

I walk this morning, rays
of sun chasing night from the clearing,
startle chipmunk & coyote, ears
failing, asleep below
the cliff, curled on the ground,
his bed one of leaves,
his fears of man unfounded where
I am concerned. In the coming rain,

poetry is a possibility.

The line

The line is nothing without the page.
Its white space lures the poet

into the folds of a woman's eyes
into some secret unfurling there

as easy to miss
as a snowflake on Jack's Knob

on a night when clouds
cover the light of stars

cover the moon
that time

when the north wind steals
the very warmth

the poet seeks.

The first time

I saw the bobcat,
it stopped in the center
of the lane
in front of the car,
blinded
& I braked to a stop.

How wild it was!
How frightened...
I thought it beautiful
the first time I saw it.

Before a week passed,
it crossed the highway again,
white stub of a tail
& ears upright, running, gone
in an instant.
The second time I saw it,
I thought of you.

In the white space,

you hide
like a snail darter
beneath a moss covered stone
in Old Seventy Creek.
The moss, green in the shade
of sycamore & oaks,
feels like a poem
beneath bare feet.

Once, on a clear winter night
above the bridge at Mt. Union,
I watched a bat feast on gnats
swarming above the white

reflection of a full moon.

The Mexican waiter

says *Share...*
I don't understand.

You say *One order...*
One empty plate...

I say *We both will eat...*
Share the food...

He writes.
Says nothing else...

Goes away...
You lean back...

Hands on your head...
You see me

& drop your arms
then stretch again,

arms on your head,
watching me from that pose.

It is not a poem that you incite
me to write on this Monday.

I wish, instead, to be an artist not
of words, but of colors on white canvas.

It was my first brushstroke
that you saw in my eyes.

Warm December Day

I should leave my office
& look for poetry in the flowing
water that is Old Seventy Creek.

There will be ice
perhaps tonight & my muse, going
into her words, sleek,

slender, I imagine her still
to be. I have heard her voice
a dozen times or more,

tho never in the chill
of winter. I should go rejoice
by the clear water before

the next cold front hits. There
is a chance she will pass thru
the narrow valley not expecting me.

I know exactly where
the water rises & sinks—coming thru
darkness into light. She

can hide on the cliff , watching & I
will write a poem down the
slippery otter slide.

I wake to a dream

& I am a passenger
in a car.
There is a woman
behind the wheel.
The car is not moving.
Why she is not driving,
I do not know.
How long we have been stopped,
I have no idea.
I want to ask her
where we were going
& I try to look up
& see her face.
I see only the dash,
her right hand
on the arm rest,
her lap,
her waist,
the outline of a breast
& nothing more.
I want to speak,
but I don't know
whether I have a face
with a mouth
& a tongue inside,
but I have eyes
& I have a left arm
& a left leg.
It occurs to me
that I may have one eye only,
the left.
She takes my arm
& pulls it up,

& twists it back
to cup her other breast,
She has a left side
& both arms.
She reaches back
& takes my other arm
& holds my hand
for a moment.
When she squeezes it,
I feel her strength.
When she releases it,
my hand drops to my leg.
She takes my left hand
from her breast
& tucks my elbow
into the head of the valley
created by her legs.
I fear no evil
for she is with me.
I hear her breath
go out & mine go in.
Then I wake to a dream in a place
where I have never been
& she has not deserted me.
She lies beside me on a bed
on her back
& on her stomach
are words I recognize as the poem
I should have written on a woman's
white skin once in some other life.

Watching my sister

draw the cover for my book,
I see how she takes things
that are hidden behind white
sketch paper & gives form
to you tho she has no idea
what you look like.

To write poetry,
I had to learn to see what was hidden
among things that never get lost
like you naval exactly where it is
or your breasts or Old Seventy Creek
where it is & where wild ginseng grows.

& Whitman watching his New Orleans girl
& loving her became a different man
& a better poet
& she, his driving force, who can know
what became of her or which words he
wrote for her & which words he penned for
a young man who loved him

whom he loved?
& me in Wal-Mart feeling watched
& looking up into the eyes of a young
woman watching me
& she looks neither away nor scans items
tho customers stand in a long line

& I ask myself if I am supposed to know
her or if she is supposed to know me
& I ask myself if I am destined to meet her
& I ask myself if I see me in her
or if she sees herself in me
& I smile at her & she almost smiles

Now watching myself write words
across the page & down
Now thinking how there is a driving force
in me equal to the force that pushes
Old Seventy Creek up & out of the ground
to flow

Now thinking & feeling the body of a
woman I have never felt as lover
Now moving my fingers down her face
I cannot touch
to kiss her lips
with the tips of my fingers again

& now wondering if anyone will read my
words & understand me the way some
readers read my words & understand
themselves, I hesitate
& now closing my eyes I see you
without a shred of rhyme

& being no artist of straight lines
I begin to draw the curves
the bends
the spaces between
the immeasurable depths the
hidden among things that never get lost...

Finding a poem from 1984

on the importance of language to that
which is called poetry
& on hoping that turtles need never try to
hide beside a discarded can, a poem I
remember writing to a woman—to poets—
at a time when I had found a word which
was like a woman inciting me to write.

Poets shape words into a poem—push
them along lines as much by feel as by
rules, & the woman, afraid to push
feelings, would have the poet wait in the
present for something that had already
come to be in a moment by a creek
that came out of the ground like Old
Seventy Creek rises.

The poet took the woman in search of
poetry
to that place where the flow sinks fast
& rises on the other side of a hill
not a mountain more cold than cool
the way words sometimes rise from the
mind—from the touch of another.

The fry, the frog, and the lines in the mud
seemed real but rhyme hid internal unlike
striders skimming the surface of a clear
pool—unlike the birds singing. Clouds
remained elsewhere on that day
& a Monarch butterfly circled near her
cheek,

so much like words becoming
reality in the illusion
called life—becoming illusion in reality
we swam
& the woman asked *does this place*
continue to exist when no one visits?
I chose not to answer for the truth was I
wanted to retire within her & write
for a long time, even rhyme
if I chose,

but we went forth from that place
in many directions at the one
& the same time, confronting the
strangers we let ourselves become there.
The climb
up toward the summit & the plateau
became a turned page
& the entrance to the woman became a
line, an open gate where travelers stop
without being told not to trespass.
I remember these many years later
how blue her eyes were on that morning
& how blue the water was
& the sky, most especially her eyes.

Second poem from 1984

It was not difficult for me
to learn how not to tilt
at windmills

or appear less vain
in reality
than in illusion

For need of a word
a poem becomes prose
a problem for the poet

I would become—
the man I was already.
Heart beating to the rhythm

of a dancer's feet,
I wrote like Keats,
exerting authority over words

& sleeping naked
in your bed
when you would have me

December 31, 2006 before it rains

I sit reading & I hear it,
a sound out of place,
outdoors.

I go outside
& stand on the deck,
listening.

Wind chimes play
but their sounds
are not what I seek.

Toward the creek,
first right,
then to the left

an answering song.
Sun on my face,
warm as late April

teases me
& confuses the frogs.
I hear wind toward the south

its voice threatening.
I inhale slowly.
I am not poet enough

to craft
a more beautiful
morning.

I will write

myself into some place
where I am waking,
looking for a poem
hidden
among things
that never get lost.

I don't remember who said
a poet must walk, visioning
always.
Perhaps the saying was a poet's words,
& I, reading, slipped on them as tho
they were slick rocks
in Old Seventy Creek.

I once lived a poem
far from Kentucky.
I remember well it was on Santorini
& riding up from the cruise ship,
a woman on a donkey
smiled at me.
I knew in that moment the Greek
leading the animal was not Joseph
& those long, tan legs
were not Mary's.